The Genie King

A Magical World Awaits You
Read

THE
SECRETS
OF
DROON

THE SECRETS OF DROON

— TONY ABBOTT —

The Genie King

Illustrated by Royce Fitzgerald
Cover illustration by Tim Jessell

SCHOLASTIC INC.
New York Toronto London Auckland
Sydney Mexico City New Delhi Hong Kong

For those who have been here since the beginning

For more information about the continuing saga of Droon,
please visit Tony Abbott's website at
www.tonyabbottbooks.com

ISBN 978-0-545-09884-7

12 11 10 9 8 7 6 5 4 3 2 1   10 11 12 13 14 15/0

Printed in the U.S.A.   40
First printing, June 2010

Contents

One

Turban Tricks

It was the end of a long school day, it was sweltering in the classroom, it was the final minute of math review, and it was so boring that Neal Kroger had to close his eyes.

Just for a second, he said to himself. *A tiny rest. It's not like anyone will miss me.*

The instant Neal's eyelids drooped, his desk, his friend Julie, the entire classroom around him, and the whole bustling school seemed to vanish.

Even *he* vanished, because when he closed his eyes, he wasn't Neal Kroger anymore.

He was Zabilac, supreme high leader of the magical Genies of the Dove!

And he was on a mission.

"We have one goal, and one only!" he intoned, his voice echoing thunderously across the sand dunes of the Crimson Desert. "We must save Eric Hinkle!"

"Yes, Zabilac!" his six genie companions replied.

Neal was daydreaming, but he truly *was* a genie. In fact, Zabilac, as he had named himself, had turned out to be the legendary First Genie of the Dove, head of a league of seven time-traveling magicians who were among the most powerful of all of Droon's magical folk.

Powerful, yes. Magical, yes.

Although . . .

Neal hadn't performed very many real spells yet. He was still learning the hundreds of spells in his genie scroll, and so far he'd mastered only the easier tricks all genies could perform.

He wished he could learn true genie powers soon.

He needed them.

Droon needed them, too.

Not long before, Neal's oldest and dearest friend, Eric Hinkle, had been wounded, poisoned, cursed, and magically transformed into the evil Prince Ungast.

As Ungast, Eric was now in the service of Gethwing, the fearsome moon dragon and leader of the beast armies of the Dark Lands.

Real genie powers were needed to

stop Gethwing. Real genie powers could save Eric.

And that, in the final minute of math class, was Neal's single mission — to save Eric.

"Genies, are you with me?" he boomed as the desert winds wafted across his sunlit face.

"Now and forever, Zabilac!" said Hoja, the clever Seventh Genie, his plump face peeking happily out from under a giant red turban.

"Then follow me over the dunes —"

"Except," Hoja interrupted. "Shouldn't we find the Moon Medallion first?"

The Moon Medallion?

Three days earlier, Eric had asked his friends to find the legendary Moon Medallion. Eric said he needed it to defeat Gethwing.

"I nearly forgot about the Medallion," said Neal. "Of course we need it. So, fine. We locate the Medallion and save Eric. Are we ready?"

"With all respect, Zabilac, we can't forget Galen," said Anusa, the beautiful Second Genie. "We need him in this battle."

Of course Neal hadn't forgotten Galen! Galen Longbeard was the greatest wizard in the history of Droon and a dear friend to Neal, Eric, and the others. After Galen had hidden the Medallion, he had been kidnapped and spirited away by a mysterious woman pretending to be Anusa.

Neal nodded. "So we've got three goals. Rescue Galen, find the Moon Medallion, save Eric. But that's all. Genies, get ready to fly —"

"But Lord Sparr is attacking Zorfendorf Castle!" said Jyme, the long-gowned, white-haired genie who was sometimes old, sometimes young, and always beautiful. "We must discover why."

Neal grumbled, but he knew that Jyme, too, was right. "Fine. We have four very big goals. Does anyone else —"

Fefforello, a genie with a thick mustache, raised his slender hand. "Excuse me, Master Zabilac. Droon's magical cities are falling to Gethwing one by one. Which city shall we save first?"

Neal cleared his throat. "Are there any more goals to add to the list —"

"Snibble-ibble? Plim-plum?" The twin baby genies, River and Stream, giggled in unison.

Neal sighed.

Even in his daydreams, things were never easy.

"Yes, of course, but we have to save Eric!" cried Neal. "And we're doing that first!"

"Zabilac has spoken!" said Hoja. "Everyone, prepare! Doves, assemble!"

At Hoja's command, hundreds of white doves fluttered like a giant warbling cloud over Neal's head. Meanwhile, a vast army of fearsome beasts was marching across the valley below.

"Genies," said Neal, "into battle!"

Raising his arms like wings, he launched himself over the dunes. No sooner had he dipped into the desert valley than a band of gray-furred wingwolves swooped down from the clouds, clawing mercilessly at him.

Neal spun like a top, moving his arms like propeller blades. "Take that! And that!" he cried, fending off their stinging claws until they scattered in disarray.

"What, is that all you've got?" Neal cried.

It was not, for next came the green-faced Goblins of Goll. They slithered from the sand as they had long ago, when they first battled young Galen upon his arrival in Droon.

Standing his ground, Neal sent forth rapid blasts of icy sparks, and the goblins shrieked and slunk back into the sand.

"But hey, I'm just getting started," said Neal.

"That's good," said Hoja. "Because here come more!"

The Seventh Genie was right. After the goblins came the Warriors of the Skorth, skeleton creatures whose bones clattered with every step. After them, swarms of snakelings and hordes of jungle foxes led the way for galloping packs of lion-headed beasts.

And there at the crest of a massive red dune, Neal saw Eric chained to a boulder.

"Eric!" he cried. "Hold on. I'm coming —"

Suddenly, Neal's toes twitched, and his scalp tingled. A dark beast was darting over the dunes.

It was Gethwing, the moon dragon.

The great creature's four wings flapped, and dark air trailed him like a foul cloud.

"It was only a matter of time before *he* showed up," Neal breathed.

With the other genies busy quelling the beast armies, it was up to him.

Securing his enormous blue turban to his head, Neal planted his feet firmly on the ground and refused to move. He had to stop the dragon there and then, or all their battles would mean nothing.

Can I defeat the dragon and free Eric?

As Gethwing approached, that was the only question on Neal's mind.

That was the question this fight would answer.

That was the question, the only question that meant anything at all, until Gethwing opened his jaws and asked another. . . .

"What is the ratio of the circumference to the diameter of a circle?"

Neal blinked. "What is the what of the what to the what?"

At once, the Crimson Desert disappeared. In fact, everything disappeared — the genies, the black-winged moon dragon, the giant blue turban, Eric, Droon, and the entire daydream.

Neal found himself at his desk in school, looking up at his teacher, Mrs. Michaels.

"Would you like me to repeat the question?" she asked.

Neal cleared his throat. "Uh . . . yes, please. In English this time."

As Mrs. Michaels repeated her question, Neal glanced over at Julie for help. Julie, however, was staring past him at the whiteboard on the front wall.

Neal, take a look! she said in the silent way the friends had learned in Droon.

"Neal?" said Mrs. Michaels.

"I'm thinking," he said. He stroked his chin and pretended to think, while really glancing at the whiteboard behind her.

He nearly fell off his chair.

Large letters were appearing one by one on the board as if traced by an invisible hand.

Whoa, Julie! he murmured.

I know! she replied.

The first letter was . . . W.

This was quickly followed by . . . O.

Then . . . N.

Then . . . no more.

W . . . O . . . N . . .

Neal's heart raced as it had in his day-dream battle against the dark forces of Droon. Had the battle been *won*? Was the coming war in Droon already over? Had Eric been saved, Galen freed, and the Moon Medallion found?

Was Gethwing finally vanquished?

Then his heart sank.

He remembered that Princess Keeah always used a code when she sent written messages from Droon to the Upper World.

The letters were to be read backward.

Her message was not WON, but NOW.

Keeah needs us, Julie said silently. **Right now!**

"Neal, the answer?" said Mrs. Michaels, growing impatient. "I'm waiting."

Suddenly — *brnnnng!* — the dismissal bell rang, and everyone jumped from their seats.

"Saved by the bell!" Neal said, leaping to his feet.

"Not so fast, Neal," said Mrs. Michaels. "I'd like you to stay after school today. You'll need to know the answer for tomorrow's test."

"Stay after?" said Neal. "But the bus —"

"You can catch the late bus," she said. "I'll meet you back here in five minutes."

"Oh, this is so not good," Neal grumbled.

"No kidding, Einstein," said Julie, glaring at him as she gathered books from her desk. "You-know-who needs us in you-know-where at exactly you-know-when!"

Neal's genie sense flickered. "Wait a second. I just read about a genie trick to help us zip back to a few minutes ago. I can use it to answer the question right the first time. Then, when the bell rings, we're out of here!"

Julie blinked. "That might actually work."

"Sure it will," he said. "*If* you tell me the answer to . . . whatever the teacher asked."

"We already studied this," she said, pulling him into the hallway with her. "The ratio of the circumference of a circle to its diameter is called pi."

Instinctively, Neal glanced toward the cafeteria. "Pie? Really? What flavor? Full crust or crisscross? With ice cream?"

Julie shook her head. "It's about the dimensions of a *circle*, and the answer is pi —"

"I get it! Because a pie is a circle of food."

"No!" said Julie. "Because they call the formula by the old Greek letter pi."

Neal nodded. "Wait. Are you saying the pie is old? So what? Pie is pie. Wow, I'd love some gizzleberry pie right now. Which reminds me of Droon —"

"Which is where we need to be right now!" said Julie.

"Neal?" Mrs. Michaels called from the classroom.

"Coming!" he said. "Okay, Julie, hold on to your backpack and check out this cool genie trick."

As soon as the hall emptied, Neal tugged his enormous blue turban out of his pocket and slipped it onto his head. He searched his scroll, found the charm, and spoke the words.

"Bolly-molly-hip-snoo!"

With a *whoosh* and a *squeak*, Neal and Julie were back at their desks, the classroom was full, and it was one minute before the bell.

As she had only moments before, Mrs. Michaels stepped over to Neal's desk and asked, "What is the ratio of the circumference to the diameter of a circle?"

Neal grinned. "That's easy. Cake!"

"Excuse me?" said Mrs. Michaels.

He glanced at Julie. ***Oh, no! I forgot!***

It's a foreign word! said Julie.

"Danish!" said Neal.

Mrs. Michaels sighed. "I don't think so —"

"Napoleon!"

"Neal, I'd like you to —"

"Strudel!"

"— stay after today —"

Last clue — gizzleberry! Julie hissed.

"Pie!" said Neal.

Brnnnnng!

The bell rang, Mrs. Michaels stepped aside, the classroom emptied, and Neal and Julie rushed for the bus.

"I can't believe you pulled that off!" she said when they dived into their seats. "It must be such a mess inside that head of yours."

"No, actually," Neal said as the bus drove away. "It's like a very neat counter display. The doughnuts are next to the muffins, which are next to the cakes, which are next to the pies. It's very orderly."

Julie shook her head. "That's kind of sad."

"Tell me about it," he said. "Every time I *think*, I get *hungry*, so I have to *stop* thinking and find a *snack*. It's a vicious circle."

She sighed. "Too bad you don't know the circumference of it. Here's Eric's corner."

When the bus pulled to a stop and the door opened, the two friends jumped off into Eric's yard and ran for his side door. They dashed down the kitchen stairs and stuffed themselves into the basement closet.

"I hope we can help today," said Julie, reaching for the bulb and pulling the chain.

"No kidding," said Neal. "It's getting very dangerous. Not to mention complicated."

Whoosh! The floor beneath their feet suddenly vanished. In its place stood the top step of a staircase coiling down through Droon's sky. The stairway seemed made of light, each step shimmering up at them as they made their way down.

"So many things to do," Julie said.

"I know," said Neal, wondering if any of the goals in his daydream would be accomplished today. But it didn't matter.

He knew which one was first.

Save Eric!

Two

On the Roof of the World

Swirling pink clouds parted as Neal and Julie descended the stairs. Soon the full beauty of Droon's landscape stretched out before them.

Vast expanses of grass waved in the wind, while rivers as blue as the evening sky wandered lazily toward the horizon.

"Another great day in Droon," said Julie.

"Not in all of Droon," said Neal.

Farther to the east, dense clouds hung low over the evil Dark Lands, the domain ruled by the moon dragon, Gethwing.

Watching the darkness push against the clear sky like an unstoppable force, Neal couldn't help shuddering. Over the past few days, Gethwing had seemed unstoppable, too.

"The dragon's reign is spreading faster and farther than ever," said Julie. "We have a big job to do. We'd better not fail."

"I know," Neal said. "I know."

With his big blue turban secured tightly on his head, Neal felt incredibly lucky to be Zabilac.

Genie tricks were very cool, sometimes odd, but very often the only thing that would work. He liked that. He might not have the huge powers his friends had, but tricks like turning time back a few minutes were really helpful, if he used them right.

"I wonder where Keeah wants us to meet her. And why, exactly," said Julie.

"The stairs are turning north," said Neal with a sudden shiver. "I smell snow."

Sure enough, as they emerged from the clouds, the two friends felt the sting of icy winds. The lower stairs were buried in deep drifts of snow.

"A mountain," said Julie. "But where —"

All at once, a figure covered in fur from head to foot staggered out of the snow at the base of the stairs.

"It's an ice monster!" Neal gasped. "Get back —"

But as the children struggled against the snow, a sudden gust of wind blew around the approaching figure, and its fur hood came away, revealing waves of golden blond hair.

"It's Keeah!" cried Julie. "Hurry down!"

No sooner had they jumped from the bottom step to greet Princess Keeah than Max the spider troll dragged himself out of a nearby snowbank. "Such weather! Julie, Neal, here are two Parkas by Pasha. Warm yourselves and come. The summit is this way. Follow me!"

As the friends hurried up the mountain, they spied a flash of light across the snowy sky, and the air filled with a deep growling sound.

Out of the snow came a golden chariot harnessed to a pair of black-scaled flying lizards called groggles. In the chariot was Princess Neffu, Keeah's evil opposite, who had aligned her magic with Gethwing to form the dragon's Crown of Wizards.

"Her!" said Keeah, her fingers scattering violet sparks. "Stand your ground, everyone!"

Neffu landed her chariot in a swirl of snow.

"What do *you* want *here*?" asked Julie.

"Yeah," said Neal. "Are you just here to scare us with your dirty looks?"

"Where's your army?" added Max.

Neffu's eyes were as red as the tunic she wore. She smiled coldly. "I don't need an army. I'm just here to mess with your heads!"

With that, she conjured a blazing fireball in one hand and a fiery staff in another.

"Sorry — we're not playing ball today," said Keeah. She blasted the fireball into a hundred harmless fragments.

Neffu scowled. "Now I'm not playing, either!" The dark princess summoned an even larger fireball and batted it right at Keeah.

Without thinking, Neal swept Keeah out of the way, and the fireball exploded on the rocks behind them.

"How perfectly gallant of you!" Neffu smirked. Then she swung her flaming staff at Neal. When he ducked, she leaped out of the chariot and knocked his turban into the snow.

"Look at you now, genie boy. You're utterly defenseless!" she gloated.

Julie kicked snow at Neffu, dousing the flaming staff with a sharp *hiss* and giving Neal time to scoop up his turban.

"And now I'm utterly defense*ful*!" he said.

Together, the three children and Max charged at the dark princess, but she jumped back into the golden chariot.

"Until next time!" she said, snapping the reins. The groggles groaned, then lifted the chariot into the air. With a snarl, Neffu disappeared into the whirling snow.

"That was strange, wasn't it?" said Julie. "Why did she come here? Just to bother us?"

"Of course it was strange," said Neal, fluffing his turban to its full height. "It was Neffu."

"She can't be any other way," said Keeah.

"Come on," said Max. "We're losing time."

Trekking northward toward the mountain's summit, the four friends soon found themselves in a clearing surrounded by tall peaks. The white air howled outside the peaks, but was oddly calm within them.

They had been in this place before.

"You know where we are," said Keeah. "This is where the magical Castle of

Silversnow will appear when a single word is spoken."

As she lowered her fur hood, Neal spied a small silver vial around her neck. It held a single drop of fazool, the mysterious liquid that was the poison that caused — and was the cure for — Eric's terrible curse. "We all know what that word is. Neal, care to do the honors?"

"Thanks," he said. Taking a deep breath, he spoke the word that contained such power.

"Zara!"

As soon as the name left Neal's lips, the icy surface began to tremble under their feet.

"It begins!" said Max.

Neal knew that whenever Eric spoke Zara's name, he felt a pain deep in his chest. Zara, known as the Queen of Light, was the mother of the three wizard brothers, Galen, Sparr, and Urik. She meant something special to Eric, too, though no one knew exactly what. It was one of the deepest and longest-held secrets in all of Droon.

VOOM! — the ground split open, and a jagged wall of ice shot up from below.

Voom! Voom! Voooooom! A second, third, and fourth wall appeared. Then an archway. A balcony. A flight of stairs.

Tower upon tower erupted from beneath the icy crust, and a fabulous castle grew before the children's eyes.

By the time the last parapet rumbled into place, the Castle of Silversnow stood tall and gleaming, a stout fortress of snowy white, a palace of frosty frost.

"When Galen took the Medallion from Jaffa City," Keeah said, "he hid it somewhere. Inside this castle is a magic room.

In it, if we are lucky, we'll discover where the Medallion is!"

"I hope it tells us *when* the Medallion is, too," said Julie. "In my vision, Galen said no one would find it in a hundred years."

"If I know my master," said Max, "that is a riddle we must solve. If we cannot, then our friend Eric will be lost, and so will Droon itself. Come to the doors. Let us enter!"

Neal trembled to hear someone say the word he would barely let himself think.

Lost.

Ever since they first crashed their tricycles into each other, he and Eric had been the closest of friends. In school, at home, hanging around, they were always together, always joking.

The day the two boys and Julie discovered Droon and met Keeah, they had become as close as four people could be.

Neal felt they were a family, meant to stay together always.

When Eric became a wizard, Neal was thrilled. He knew his friend deserved amazing powers more than anyone else. Eric was destined for great and wonderful things.

The idea that his best friend might be lost — *lost* — sent a chill down his spine. He would fight to the death to bring Eric back.

At the big wooden doors of the icy castle, Keeah took a large iron knocker into both hands, raised it, then let it fall.

THOOM! The sound echoed through the halls within. Soon the children heard footsteps, then the creaking of ancient hinges, then the doors swinging wide.

Standing inside was a giant dressed from his boots to his helmet in dented, rusty armor.

"Old Rolf!" said Max. "Greetings!"

With an enormous hand, Old Rolf, the leader of the famous Knights of Silversnow, patted each of them on the shoulder.

"Enter our humble abode!" he said with a bow. "I know why you are here. Long ago, Galen built a secret room in Silversnow to speak with his long-lost mother, Queen Zara. This room is known as the Winter Room."

Outside a door at the end of the hall stood the two other knights, Lunk and Smee. Like Rolf, both wore old battle armor.

Nodding in unison, the three knights took hold of three identical knobs and turned them. The moment the big door opened, snowflakes drifted from the ceiling, cascading onto a little stool carved completely out of ice.

Neal trembled. "The Winter Room!"

"The meditation stool is magic," said Lunk. "Tried it once myself. Fell asleep. Froze to the stool." As he looked at the stool, he yawned.

So did Smee and Rolf. Neal remembered that the knights were usually asleep and woke only when they were needed.

"Julie, try to remember as much of your vision of Galen as you can," said Keeah. "We need a clue to help us solve his riddle and find the Medallion."

"Julie, if you please," said Rolf, "sit on the stool and close your eyes. That's how Galen used to do it."

"You'll feel the wizard," said Smee. "His age-old spirit will commune with yours. Look around in your trance. Try to see everything."

Julie sat on the stool and closed her eyes. At first, her features were calm. Then her eyelids began to flutter. "Smoke . . .

purple smoke everywhere," she murmured. "Like a kind of . . . visible . . . perfume . . . and . . . light. . . ."

"What else do you see?" asked Keeah.

Julie's face darkened. "Galen . . . I see him. . . ." She shook her head. "It's already fading!"

"Maybe I can help," said Neal. "I read something in my scroll. There's a trick. . . ."

He paused, noting his use of the word trick again. Why didn't he call them powers the way Julie, Keeah, or Eric always did?

"Just be careful," said Julie.

"I always am," said Neal, even though he knew he wasn't *always* careful.

A moment later, Neal felt himself drifting out of his body and into a bright room with floor-to-ceiling bookshelves. It looked just like a library. When he turned, he saw a lettered sign that read JULIE'S BRAIN.

Neal's chest fluttered. "This is so cool!"

Then he saw Julie herself, walking toward him from the other side of the room.

"I know the book you want," she said.

"You do?"

"It's a memory I can't quite reach," she said. "The purple book. Way up there." She pointed to a high shelf. "Please hurry!"

With a nod, Neal crossed his arms and floated up to the shelf. He removed the purple book, opened it, and began to read.

"'Galen appeared with wisps of purple smoke on his shoulders, cloak, and hat. He walked as if he were pushing his way out of purple flame. Only it wasn't flame, and it wasn't hot. It was perfumed smoke. Galen said he stole the Moon Medallion. Then he said, "To keep it safe . . . none shall

lay eyes upon it . . . for a hundred years!" Just before he faded away, Galen said one more thing. . . .'"

Neal had to squint because the letters were so tiny. Concentrating on Julie's memory, he was finally able to read the word.

"Twins," he said. "Galen said 'twins.'"

Purple smoke? A hundred years? Twins?

"I've got it!" Neal said.

In a flash, the bright little library of Julie's brain vanished, and both he and Julie were back in the Winter Room with everyone else.

Blinking her eyes open, Julie glared at him. "Neal, were you just rummaging around inside my head?"

He grinned. "I wiped my feet before I went in," he said. "But thanks to you, I discovered where the Medallion is. Purple smoke was one clue. A hundred years was another. Twins was the third. Together they mean only one thing."

"Please don't say pie," said Julie.

Neal's stomach pinched for an instant. "No, they mean . . . the City of Ut. You remember Ut, right? Its walls are made of purple smoke. It appears only once every hundred years. And its rulers, Duke Snorfo and Duchess Dumpella, are exact twins of the two of us. Galen was in Ut when he hid the Moon Medallion!"

Duke Snorfo was indeed Neal's exact twin. They looked identical, though Snorfo had a bad attitude. On the other hand, Snorfo's sister, Dumpella, resembled Julie exactly, and she was as nice as could be. The Duke and Duchess's resemblance to Neal and Julie had caused a lot of confusion the first time the children were in Ut.

"The City of Ut?" said Max. "The city in the bottle? The city on the Saladian Plains?"

"All of the above," said Neal, nodding. "All we need is the magic bottle of Ut, and a little genie trick I know, and we'll be in and out of the city in a flash."

Julie smiled. "For the second time today, I'm forced to say that might actually work."

"And . . . you're welcome," said Neal.

"The bottle containing Ut is hidden safely in Galen's vanishing tower," said Max. "It lies on the plains at the foot of the Ice Hills of Tarabat!"

"Let's go get the sled!" said Rolf.

"I guess we're going to Ut," said Keeah.

"To Ut!" said Julie.

"To Ut!" said Neal. "By way of Galen's tower!"

Three

The Eye of the Storm

A loud shriek brought them to the castle doors. In the swirling snow overhead, they spied a dense swarm of winged beasts.

"Wingwolves," said Julie. "Not good."

Rolf licked his finger, stuck it in the air, and silently calculated the wolves' flight plan. "If I'm not mistaken, those beasties are headed directly for the Saladian Plains."

"Right where Ut is," said Julie.

"Sounds like you'll be wanting some backup," said Lunk. "You need us knights!"

Smee clapped his large hands together. "Ooh, I feel like wrestling a wolfie or three."

"It will soon be noon," said Rolf. "But I'm ready for a little knight music."

"The snow is picking up again," said Max.

"Not to worry," said Rolf. "Our sled will take you to Galen's tower. After that, we're off to the Saladian Plains!"

"Let's do it," said Keeah.

The three knights tramped around the side of the castle to an enormous wooden sled that sat under an icy arch like a car in a garage. Ten feet long from stem to stern, the sled had two sets of runners on each side and sported wings that coiled up like crazy antlers.

"So very cool," said Neal. "Who made it?"

Smee blushed. "It's my design, thankee."

Lunk patted the sled's seats. "Climb in."

Once they were all in, Rolf loosed the brake, pushed a lever, and the sled leaped into the snow, careening away from the great frosty castle and down the Ice Hills of Tarabat.

They sped across the plains, traveling southwest at great speed toward the thick mass of trees known as the Farne Woods.

Finally, the sled slowed, and Max jumped up in his seat. "Oh, it's good to see these woods again! Hidden among the trees is Galen's invisible tower. All we must do now . . . is find it."

"We'll leave that to you," said Rolf. "We're sledding right to the Plains of

Saladia. We'll meet you there. Smee, old chap, set the course, if you please."

Smee engaged several levers. "Ready."

"And we're off!" said Lunk.

With a great *whoosh* of snow, the sled bounced over the plains and out of sight.

"Let's head into the trees," said Julie, scanning the sky. "Time is passing quickly."

Together the children and Max entered the Farne Woods. Almost at once, the sounds of the forest took over, creaking and sighing and breathing like an ancient person. A friend.

"I'll never forget the first time I saw Galen's invisible tower," said Neal. The wizard's vanishing tower was fashioned from the trunk of a giant tree that had turned to stone over hundreds of years. "I didn't even *see* it. I *felt* it. When it smashed my poor nose."

Neal smiled, remembering how that

had happened on his first day in Droon. The memory made him think of Eric again.

Keeah smiled, too. "Maybe we should send you in first, Neal. I see an empty clearing just ahead. Maybe it's not exactly empty?"

Neal knew they could spend hours trying to find the invisible tower. "Okay, leave it to me," he said. "Besides, it's only a nose."

Pulling his turban tight, Neal moved into a broad clearing among the trees. His friends hung back and watched him slowly enter.

It was fine, really.

Neal knew he was the funny one. Always hungry. A little silly. Sometimes forgetful. Often afraid. It was just how he was. Being a genie was also a bit funny. You had odd powers. You could levitate, but not fly long distances. You could travel in time, but had to have your turban on to do it. You had sharp senses, but were easily distracted.

But as Neal stepped forward into the empty air, he also knew he was more than a funny kid with a stomach that was always empty.

Like now, for instance.

Remembering his first day in Droon led to thinking about everything that had happened since. The more he remembered, the heavier his heart felt.

Eric had been Prince Ungast for only a short while, and yet it seemed so long since they'd joked around together.

As he made his way forward, Neal knew he'd give anything to have things back the way they were. It *could* happen.

Maybe by the end of the day they would see Eric.

Maybe he would even — *wham!*

Neal staggered back as a flash of pain shot through his face. "Owww!"

An instant later — *shooom!* — a massive tower rippled into view.

Max jumped. "Yes! Great job, Neal!"

"You found it!" said Julie.

Neal rubbed his nose. "No problem. The nose always knows."

As quickly as they could, the four friends raced up the tower's spiraling passages to the room at the top, where Max leaped to a high shelf and clasped a glass bottle etched with strange symbols.

"The bottle of Ut!" he exclaimed gleefully. "Just where Galen left it!"

His nose still aching, Neal gazed in awe at the purple smoke swirling inside the glass. He knew that the entire City of Ut — one of the five magic cities of Droon — lay inside the bottle, waiting to emerge.

"It's like a living snow globe," said Julie. "Beautiful in its own way."

"We'll soon be walking its streets," said Keeah. "We have until sunset to find the Medallion and get back out. I suggest we fly one of Pasha's magic carpets. There's no faster way to the Saladian Plains."

Among Galen's collection was a narrow red carpet with yellow fringes. Wasting no time, Neal, Julie, Keeah, and Max clambered on board and zoomed out of the tower.

For the next hour, the carpet raced across the skies. When they spied the hilly plains east of Bangledorn Forest, the friends knew they had arrived in Saladia.

"The bottle of Ut has to be placed on its exact spot or the city won't appear," said Neal, gazing at the purple bottle. "One inch to the left or right, and Ut won't come. Max, the map."

"Have it right here," said the spider troll.

He quickly unrolled an ancient map he had brought from Galen's tower.

Holding a pen in each of six of his eight legs, Max sketched a few lines on the map, starting from the edge and working to the center. All the lines met at a single point.

"There!" he said, pointing to a shallow valley midway between three dusty hills.

Neal peered down at the spot Max had located. The same wingwolves they had seen flying over Silversnow had joined with others. Now they numbered in the thousands.

"Okay, look," Neal said. "Ut usually appears once every century. The sun strikes the bottle, it shakes like crazy, and out it comes. Today, we'll need a temporary spell to make it appear. I'm pretty sure there's one in my scroll."

"While you conjure Ut, I'll create a shield to keep the wingwolves out," said Keeah.

"And I'll create a dust storm," said Julie.

Max wheeled the carpet around. They bounced once and landed under one of the three hills out of sight of the wolfen army. Over the rise they spotted the Knights of Silversnow, their sled flying as if on the wings of the wind. While Smee and Lunk waved their clubs high in the air, Rolf boomed a laugh.

"Onward! To the ridge!" he called. "Let no beasties harm our heroes!"

The three giant knights plowed right into battle with the wingwolves.

"And now — Ut!" said Max.

Julie jumped into the air and began to fly around in a wide circle. A wall of dust grew in her wake. It rose higher and higher, allowing Keeah time to work her magic.

Bowing her head and raising her arms high, the princess chanted until a nearly

invisible shield of light formed between her hands.

"That's it!" said Max, jumping up and down. "You're doing it! Now, Neal!"

With Max's map in hand, Neal set the bottle on the exact spot and spoke the words he'd found in his tiny scroll. The little purple bottle began to shake. It wobbled. It trembled.

"Everyone, stand back!" he said.

All at once — *pop!* — the cork shot out. Max leaped and caught it as blasts of purple smoke billowed from the bottle's spout.

Neal had seen this once before — they all had — but the sight astonished him in a way few things could, for there, right before his eyes, the plains that were even now ravaged by battle gave way to giant purple walls.

"Here it comes!" he cried. "The City of Ut!"

Four

Among the Magic Streets

Jumping out of the way, Neal watched the fanciful swirls and coiling waves of smoke slow and harden into purple stone.

Walls and towers, bridges, parapets, and ramparts — all billowed up from the bottle's spout and became as solid as the plains around them.

It was beautiful. It was exciting.

It was the magic of Droon!

How he wished Eric were there to see it.

"Ut may be the most amazing of all magic cities," said Max. "It is certainly the purplest. O city of adventure. O city of the unknown!"

"O city of danger!" said Keeah, scanning its tilted towers and leaning bridges. "We have to be careful every moment we're inside Ut. Everyone up the walls and over!"

Together, the four friends scaled the walls, hand over hand, from ledge to rampart, from foothold to parapet, all the way to the summit.

With a final gesture, the princess tossed her hands up, and the magical shield she had been summoning expanded over their heads like a giant umbrella. "No one can enter Ut as long as this shield is in place."

But there was a moment as she tossed

the glittering shield from her fingertips, just a moment, when Neal saw a streak of light cross the sky.

An instant later, a twinkle of light skittered along a far wall. It was there for only a second before it turned toward them and vanished.

"I think someone entered the city with us," said Neal. "I didn't see who or what it was."

The princess breathed deeply. "I saw it, too. Magic isn't perfect, even magic performed by great wizards, and I'm still a student."

"Could it be an intruder?" asked Julie.

Max grumbled. "Perhaps we are not alone in seeking the Medallion. I predict we'll meet up with this intruder before our day is over."

"I predict a *lot* will happen before our day is over," said Julie, peering at the teeming streets below. "We have six hours before sunset. Maybe we should disguise ourselves as locals so we can move among them unnoticed."

Keeah pointed to a crowded alley below. "That market will have clothing."

"I have a pouch of coins," said Max. "We can outfit ourselves. Everyone for dress up?"

"How's this for some genie fashion?" said Neal. He removed his turban and refashioned it into a small hat. It was still blue and dotted with jewels, but no longer bore the slightest resemblance to his usual genie headgear.

Together, the four friends made their way down from the wall, dropping finally into the alley of shops, where they kept to the shadows until they came to a shop festooned with robes, scarves, shirts, hats, and capes.

The frog-faced, three-eared shop owner smiled as they tried on this and that. Neal slipped a blue tunic on over a pair of silky orange boots, while Keeah found a rose-colored cape and Julie a lilac gown trimmed with silver fringe. Max wrapped himself in a cloak of pale blue with a matching feathered hat.

"Ah, the traditional look," said the frog-faced creature, holding up a single paw with every finger extended.

"Seven coins, Max," Keeah said. "Plus tip."

Max drew ten coins from his pouch and left them on the counter. The seven-fingered stall owner smiled from ear to ear to ear.

"Let's circle the outer streets first," whispered Keeah. "If we sense nothing, we'll know Galen hid the Medallion in the heart of the city."

"Agreed," said Max. "We'll make sure it doesn't fall into the wrong hands —"

"Or the wrong *claws*," said Julie. "I sense Gethwing's presence wherever we go. He may even count Snorfo among his subjects."

"And his guards," whispered Neal. "I think I hear them stomping this way. Into the shadows, everyone. Let's not tangle with them until we have to."

Sure enough, a band of tall guards swept into the alley, sending citizens crowding into the shadows. The guards' hooded cloaks hid their faces entirely, except for the glow of their searching eyes. Each carried a large net woven of iron thread.

"The collectors," Julie whispered as the guards pushed their way through the alley.

Soon, the stomping boots of the guards faded, and the alley bustled noisily to life again. To Neal, though, one sound remained constant: the unmistakable patter of footsteps moving behind them.

Not too close, not too far.

Thip . . . thip . . .

The children moved on to another alley and then another, when suddenly, Keeah stopped. She narrowed her eyes at a street curving away on their left.

"What is it, Princess?" asked Max.

"I feel something," she said. "A kind of tug on my mind. I feel as though the Medallion is there, hidden down that little street."

"Wait a second," said Julie, turning away and stepping to the right. "Isn't it this way?"

Max trembled. "With all due respect," he said, peering into the crowd ahead, "I think you're both wrong. It's obviously hidden beyond the main square!"

Neal felt the same thing, a pull on him, almost as if the Medallion had a voice and it was calling him. But the voice wasn't coming from any of the places his friends had indicated.

"Sorry, people. It's there!" He pointed to a tall turret coiling over the center of the city.

Max blinked. "Oh, please! How can one thing be in so many places at once?"

Keeah laughed. "But of course it can! To keep the Medallion safe, Galen divided it into its four parts and hid each one in a different location. Each of us senses a different part of the Medallion."

She whispered a spell, and an image of the Moon Medallion hovered in the air before them. Flicking her fingers at the image, she made it split into its four parts.

The silver frame of the Medallion was shaped like a full moon. It moved toward

Keeah. Floating out from its center was the Pearl Sea, a tiny glimmering globe whose milky interior ebbed and flowed like waves. That hovered near Julie. Next to it was Galen's Ring of Midnight, as large in circumference as a door knocker. It went to Max.

And spinning slowly in the air, its points flashing with light, was the Twilight Star, fashioned only recently by Lord Sparr. It whirled over Neal's head.

"There are four parts and four of us," he said. "We can each find one."

Julie smiled. "Your math skills have improved since class this afternoon."

Which only made Neal think of pie, and he saw once more the bakery counter of his mind, but he quickly brushed it away and focused on the Medallion again.

Or tried to.

Thomp! Thomp!

The narrow street echoed with the sound of heavy boot steps. Before the kids could move, the guards were there.

"Halt!" boomed a voice.

Everyone froze where they stood, and the guards' deep hoods swiveled slowly from right to left and back again as they scanned the crowd.

Neal felt the guards' eyes penetrate his very bones. He was ready to cast an invisibility spell over himself and his friends when, one by one, the guards' heads stopped moving.

With a single motion, the crowd shifted away until the children stood alone in the center of the street.

"Uh-oh," Neal whispered.

"Intruders!" the voice cried. "Get them!"

Five

Scouring the City

"Split up!" shouted Keeah. "They can't catch all four of us at once!"

"We can try!" yelled the leader of the guards. "Split up and follow them!"

With a squeak, Max clambered straight up a wall to a rooftop and scrambled away. Keeah dived through the crowd and raced down a side alley, while Julie launched herself and flew across the street to a nearby bridge.

Neal glanced in every direction, then dashed to the nearest corner and concealed himself behind a crooked pillar. Retying his hat into a long cape and wrapping it around himself, he sucked in his stomach to make himself as thin as he possibly could.

He waited for the guards to leave. And waited. And waited. Then someone kicked his foot. He looked down. Julie's face glanced up at him.

"How did you get here?" he whispered.

"Me? What are *you* doing here?" she said, kicking him again. "Playing hide-and-seek with your guards?" She kicked him again.

"Julie, cut it out," he whispered. "And what do you mean, *my guards*?"

"Julie?" she said. "I'm not Julie."

"If you're not Julie . . ." Neal stared

at Julie's face until his brain clicked. "Dumpella?"

"Nealie?"

All at once, a voice bellowed down from above. "GUARDS, FIND THOSE KIDS!"

"Get down," whispered Dumpella, pulling Neal to his knees. "Here comes my brother. Wait till you see him!"

Duke Snorfo did come. But instead of his usual ornate carriage and pilkas — *whoosh-voom!* — the boy with the face identical to Neal's flew overhead on a big red genie urn.

"Whoa!" Neal said. "How can he do that?"

"Magic," said Dumpella. "And look what he's got on."

Duke Snorfo, scowling under a too-large purple crown, was wearing a wild suit and cape that looked as if he'd raided

his sister's dress-up box. At Snorfo's loud command, his dog-faced guards began searching every nook and cranny in the alley.

"Guards, FOLLOW the bouncing URN," Snorfo snarled. "If you CAN!"

Watching Snorfo hover over the streets, Neal knew that Dumpella was right — only magic could give him power over a genie urn.

Has he already found part of the Medallion?

"Nothing here," Snorfo shouted. "SEARCH the MARKET!" Both the urn-riding duke and his guards moved to another part of the city, and the street filled with people once more.

"All clear," Dumpella said.

Emerging from behind the column, Neal and Dumpella hugged, which so surprised them that they both jumped back.

Nervous, Neal spoke before he thought. "So, Dumpella, what's been going on?"

Then he remembered something about Dumpella that he had forgotten.

She talked.

Nonstop.

"Aren't you a dear for asking!" she began. "Let me tell you, it's been some roller-coaster ride since you were last here. My brother, Snorfy, says there is a kind of new magic in Ut and it's calling to him and he's searching everywhere for it but he can't find it all. I think he's flipped his crown. And don't get me started on his outfit. His magic suit, he calls it. It clashes with everything. But does he care? Not a bit. All that matters to him is finding whatever magic stuff he's talking about —"

The more Dumpella chattered on, the more Neal realized that Snorfo must already have found a piece of the Medallion.

"— the whole thing is dumb," she went on. "Snorfo just wants me out of the way so he can do his magic quest, but you know me, I'm not that kind of duchess, so I say to him, listen, brother, I tell him —"

"Dumpella," Neal interrupted, "we only have until sundown. I'm pretty sure my friends and I are searching for same thing your brother is."

"Really?" said the duchess.

"And it's way too powerful for Snorfo," Neal said. "Will you help us find it first?"

She grinned, then blushed. "You bet, Nealie! But we'll have to lie low. With that crazy urn, Snorfo gets everywhere fast."

"Let's collect my friends," said Neal.

Within a few minutes, they had found Keeah, Max, and Julie all hiding safely out of sight under a footbridge.

"The duke sounds quite obsessed," said Max after he heard Dumpella's story.

"Tell me about it," the duchess said. "Magic is all he ever talks about. And our poor people. Boy, have they been grumbling. It's a lot for a poor duchess to handle. . . ."

As Dumpella rambled on — and on — Neal realized that their search for the pieces of the Moon Medallion was going nowhere fast.

"Excuse me, Dumpella," he said. "Do you recall a wizard being here a few days ago?"

The duchess frowned. "Red suit. Snow on his boots. Sack of toys over his shoulder?"

The children looked at one another.

"No," they said together.

"How about a guy with a long cloak of stars and moons on it? He was with a lady —"

"That's Galen!" said Julie. "Only

that was no lady. It was an impostor! A kidnapper!"

"Our friend Galen managed to hide four very powerful magic things in Ut," said Max.

"I'll show you what we mean," said Keeah.

The princess whispered her spell, and the image of the Moon Medallion hovered in the air once more. As before, its four parts separated themselves. The moment the Twilight Star spun and flashed over Neal's head, Dumpella jumped.

"Snorfo has that one!" she said.

Neal nodded. "No wonder he can make the urn fly. Its magic is very powerful."

"Where does he keep the Star?" asked Julie.

"In his secret room in the palace," said the duchess. "Up there." She pointed to the highest point of the royal palace, where a tall purple tower jutted out crookedly.

"I felt it was up there," said Neal.

"All of us together should be able to find the Medallion before sunset," said Keeah.

"And if we don't?" asked Max.

"Start looking for a place to stay," said Julie. "Because we'll be here a hundred years."

"I wouldn't mind," said Dumpella, smiling at Neal.

"Gulp," he said.

"You're just saying that!" Dumpella said. "Come!"

Pressed close against the walls so that the guards crisscrossing the streets couldn't find them, the friends turned the corner and went down the street. They were as quiet as they could be.

Which was how Neal managed to hear that sound again. *Thip . . . thip . . .*

Glancing behind him, Neal tried to catch sight of their pursuer, but whoever it was stayed cleverly out of sight.

From street to street the children scurried. They soon found themselves on the north side of the vast main square. What the kids saw there made them shudder.

Lying flat in the very center of the tiled plaza was a giant stone disc. In its center stood a needle-shaped tower, pointing directly up. Neal remembered what had happened there during their first time in Ut.

The stone and the obelisk stood in the very spot where the magical Red Eye of Dawn had exploded into Ut from the Doom Gate on the other side of Droon.

"That disc must cover the hole through the earth to the Doom Gate," said Keeah.

Dumpella nodded. "It took us a long time to build that thing to cover the big hole."

The obelisk atop the disc was carved from a single length of stone fifty feet tall. At the top was a sculpture of Duke Snorfo.

"Don't get me started about *that* thing," said Dumpella. "He spent half our treasury having it built. But let's keep on. Your friend Galen traveled in the northern parts of the city."

"The Ring of Midnight is there," Max said, his eyes moist. "I sense Galen in every cobblestone in this square, in the wood of that doorway, in the canvas of that awning. Galen was here. And my heart trembles."

"Tremble it this way," said Dumpella, edging her way into the streets. "The guards will be back. And so will urn-boy."

Dumpella led them off, but Neal couldn't tear his eyes away from the obelisk.

Remembering the struggle for the Red Eye of Dawn, his mind went back to the very beginnings of his time in Droon. It was Lord Sparr's search for the Eye that first introduced him and his friends to Keeah. It was in the Doom Gate that Eric first received his powers.

Now here they were again.

Will being a genie be enough? he wondered. *I hope so. I hope so.*

"We're entering the northwest part of Ut now," said Dumpella, walking briskly out of the main square. "Nice houses on curving lanes. Notice the lawns. Very pricey."

Neal glanced from house to house, lane to lane, always looking behind him.

And there it was again.

Thip . . . thip . . .

The barely audible sound of footsteps.

They were getting closer now.

And closer still.

Six

Turnovers and Turnarounds!

"There!" said Max. "There! I feel it!" He led them down a lane on their right.

Neal knew that the hooded guards marched loudly to proclaim their power. Snorfo flew his urn noisily all around the city searching for more magic.

But someone else was simply walking. Just walking slowly behind them.

Neal turned and turned again.

Who is it? A spy? For whom? Gethwing?

All at once, Max stiffened. His legs went rigid; his orange hair stood on end.

"What is it?" asked Julie.

Slowly, Max's head turned to the left and his eyes fixed on a purple split-level house with a round purple door and a freshly cut lawn.

"Aha!" he exclaimed with a jump. "What a sly wizard our old friend is. I'd know his handiwork anywhere."

The little spider troll darted up to the front door. On it stood a silver door knocker.

Flashing a big grin, Max lifted the silver object in his paws. "It looks like a door knocker. It feels like a door knocker. Only it's not a door knocker, is it?" He tugged it once, and the object came away from the door.

"The Ring of Midnight!" said Keeah.

"One down, three to go. Only five hours until sunset," said Keeah. "We have to hurry."

"The Pearl Sea is this way," said Julie. "I'm pretty certain we're near."

Side by side with Dumpella, Julie led the friends down a series of narrow curving streets. "Here," she said, stopping short.

Neal looked into a curving alley, then turned completely around, listening. Nothing.

Had the footsteps passed, or faded, or simply stopped?

Keeah took his arm. "I hear it, too," she said. "We have to hurry. Sunset comes in a few hours. We don't want . . . complications."

Hearing voices squeaking, the children and Max crept down the alley to a corner and peeked around. Two small furry creatures were crouching next to each other on the sidewalk.

Julie slumped her shoulders. "I thought I felt something. But they're just children playing with marbles."

"Uh . . . no," said Dumpella. "Those aren't children. And those aren't marbles. They're thieves, and they're trading stolen objects."

"Perhaps one of the objects is the Pearl Sea?" asked Max. "Shall we investigate?"

"Be careful," said Keeah as they approached.

What looked at first like children turned out to be a pair of stubby old men with hairy faces and furry cloaks. One had ears like a dog, one ear up, the other down. The other wore a mustache that entirely obscured his mouth. The one with the ears looked up.

"Hey, who invited you?"

Neal held up his hands in a friendly gesture. "We're just looking for —"

"A punch in the noggin?" the dog-eared one said.

"Yeah . . . a p-p-punch in the n-n-nog-g-gin?" said the one with the mustache.

Keeah flicked her fingers, and violet sparks scattered to the sidewalk. "Let's not make this harder than it has to be. You may have something that belongs to us."

Max nodded, puffing up his chest. "Besides, Her Royal Duchess Dumpella is right here with us. I bet she has a dungeon for thieves like you."

Dumpella stepped forward. "Duchesses do have dungeons. But they also like presents. Especially pearls. I might look the other way if you let us have one."

The dog-eared thief grumbled sourly, but he opened a small treasure box filled with hundreds of shiny pearls. "Take your pick."

"T-t-take your p-p-pick," said the other.

Closing her eyes, Julie plunged her hand into the chest of pearls and suddenly gave a bright laugh. She pulled her hand out, and in her palm sat a dense, shiny pearl whose milky insides rolled slowly, like ocean waves.

"The Pearl Sea!" said Max. "The second piece found!"

"Blimey!" said the dog-eared thief. "That's my favorite!"

"M-m-my f-f-favorite," agreed the other.

"Favorite or not, it's ours now," said Dumpella. "Now, go, and thieve no more!"

The two furry creatures grumbled, but trotted away as the children darted off in search of the third piece of the Medallion.

"This is going well," said Julie. "It won't be long now. We'll be out of Ut soon enough."

Neal wasn't so sure. Things were going smoothly, but the sun was dropping and time was passing. He knew that sooner or later they'd have to get into the purple tower at the top of the palace for the Twilight Star. Was that what their follower was waiting for? For them to assemble the complete Medallion?

"There," said Keeah. "The Museum of Magic. That's where the Silver Moon is."

The princess pushed ahead in the shadows and emerged near a large marble facade. The Museum of Magic sported a single great door made of stout iron.

"Neal?" said Max.

After a quick lock-picking charm, Neal was able to tug open the door, and the friends were inside the building.

The first room was vast, high-ceilinged, and nearly completely silent. The only sound was the tiny grains of sand slipping like a golden stream from the top half of a giant hourglass.

Time is passing, Neal thought.

"This way," said Keeah softly. She led them to the next room and the one beyond that.

Finally, she paused.

This room was the largest they'd seen so far. Its marble floor seemed to stretch for miles. Its window drapes of dark red velvet, drawn tight, fell thirty feet from ceiling to sill.

Closing her eyes, Keeah raised her hand and pressed it gently to her forehead. With a sudden laugh, she spun on her heels and gasped. "Clever wizard! There it is!"

The base of the Medallion, the Silver Moon, was set in a breastplate of ceremonial armor. As twice before, the object of incredible magic was hidden in plain sight.

Keeah gently released it.

"Three out of four," said Max. "We are really getting there. Now for the fourth —"

All at once, the front door to the museum slammed open, and the quiet of the rooms was shattered. A loud flutter of feathers echoed against the walls as the single exit was blocked by a large shape wearing a cloak of feathers.

Besides that, its head was large and beaked.

Besides that, it had enormous claws.

Besides that, it was poised to attack.

Max jumped back into Keeah. "Ving? The hawk bandit? Our enemy? Here in Ut?"

The feathered creature's beak curved

into a wicked smile. "Yes, yes, yes, and . . . yes!"

Ving was leader of the fierce hawk bandits who lived in the ancient city of Tarkoom.

"Fancy meeting you here," Keeah said, her fingers beginning to spark.

"Oh, I'm fancy wherever I go," said Ving.

"And I'm even fancier," said another voice as a second hawk fluttered into the room.

It was Ming, Ving's twin sister. Leader of the just as fierce hawk pirates, Ming had more colorful feathers and wore tall black boots and a black eye patch to match.

"What are *you* doing in Ut?" asked Julie.

Ming made a face. "We were following the old wizard. Next thing you know, we're trapped in Ut with no way out. But thanks to you, we'll get out today. All we need is those shiny things you've got there."

"I don't think so," said Dumpella.

"Hey-hey!" cried a squeaky voice. "Too much grown-up talky-talky!"

Neal blinked as a third shape emerged behind Ming and Ving. This hawk creature was only a couple of feet tall, but bore the same colored feathers in the same basic pattern. He stomped toward the children, wearing impossibly big powder blue boots.

And an impossibly big diaper.

The kids staggered back.

"There's a *third* one of you?" said Julie.

"Me . . . Ing!" shouted the little hawk creature. "Them's little brother! Looky, Mingy. He has funny hat!"

"Never mind what I'm wearing," Neal snapped. "Isn't your diaper on backward?"

"Me poopy-poopy?" Ing cried, straining to look behind himself. "Vingy-Mingy fix it!"

"Your turn!" Ving and Ming said together, glaring at each other.

All of a sudden, Ing caught sight of the glittering pieces of the Medallion. "Pretty sparkles," Ing cooed. "Mine!"

"What? No!" cried Neal.

But before the children could move, Ing leaped at the three pieces of the Medallion and snatched them in his claws. Giggling, he flew up to the ceiling and circled the room.

"Now look what you've done!" Ving snapped at his sister.

"*Me?*" She scowled. "*You* taught him to grab things."

"Well, *you* taught him to fly!" said Ving.

"Just get that Medallion!" cried Keeah.

Seven

Urn Riders

In the mad scramble to get the Medallion, display cases were upended, and glass exploded everywhere. Suits of armor crashed to the floor, scattering the room with iron arms and legs. Wherever the kids turned, Ving and Ming hurled themselves in the way.

"Whatever Ing has is ours!" said Ving.

"And you can't have it!" added Ming.

"Oh, really?" said Keeah. "We'll see about

that —" She blasted at the hawks, meaning to push them out of the way, but they simply flew up and settled down unharmed.

"We can do this all day," said Ming.

"Fly, Ingy, fly!" added Ving.

"Me go!" shouted the baby bird, flapping toward the door. "With shiny things!"

Desperate to get what they'd come for, Neal cast a look around and spotted a half dozen large urns behind the hawks.

"Those are genie urns from Parthnoop!" Neal said to himself. Quickly restoring his turban to its normal shape, he whispered, "Urns — tumble!"

Instantly, the urns wobbled from side to side, then dropped to the floor and rolled at the hawk twins.

"Noooo!" yelled Ming. "Out of the —"

But the urns were moving too fast. They knocked both hawks down like bowling balls knocking down pins.

"Strike!" Neal yelped. Slowing one urn, he leaped onto it, gave it a nudge with his knees, and it lifted into the air. He dipped it toward his friends. "Everyone, climb on!"

"No fair!" cried Ving, struggling under a blue urn.

But Neal and his friends were out of the room before the hawk bandits could stagger to their feet.

Whoosh! They were out of the museum.

Voom! They were over the streets.

"Go away, muffin head!" shouted the baby hawk, swooping into a narrow street. Suddenly, his fledgling wings flapped wildly, and he tipped to one side as if weighed down.

"I think we might have caught a break!" shouted Neal. "His poopy diaper is dragging him down!"

If the baby hawk was clumsy, he was quick. From street to street he flew, his little claws clutching the Medallion tight. Finally, however, the weight of his diaper brought him closer and closer to earth.

"Mingy!" he cried over his shoulder. "Vingy! CHANGE MY DIAPEEE!!"

"Now's our chance," shouted Julie. "Get the Medallion!"

With a courage he didn't know he possessed, Neal flew the urn next to Ing and jumped off, tackling the baby hawk. They tumbled to the ground in the main square. Neal snatched the Medallion and jumped to his feet. "I have it!" he said. "And, by the way, pee-yoo!"

"Good work!" said Keeah.

"Neal, climb back on the urn," urged Max.

Julie pointed up. "Next stop, the tower —"

All at once, a shadow fell over Neal's face. He looked up. Hovering between the buildings was a fat red urn. On top of the urn sat none other than Duke Snorfo himself.

"Aha!" Snorfo yelled, jabbing his fist at Neal. "My MAGIC SEARCH is over. Gimme!"

"Neal, get back up here!" cried Keeah, urging the urn toward him.

With a snort, Snorfo dived at Neal. Clutching the Medallion tight, Neal ran as quickly as he could toward his own urn. But Snorfo swept in front of him, snatched the Medallion from him, and soared high into the air again.

"Why can't we hold on to that thing?" groaned Keeah, helping Neal back onto the urn. "Thief! You give that back!"

Duke Snorfo burst into laughter. "I'll be happy to give this thing back to you. How about . . . NEVER! Now, EXCUSE me. . . ."

Laughing like a wild man, the duke circled the vast main square and soared into the air.

"He's heading for the tower," said Dumpella. "He'll assemble the whole thing there. Then there will be *no* stopping him —"

"I'll stop him!" said Neal. His heart thundered against his chest as he urged his urn higher and faster after Snorfo.

Over the streets they flew, Neal and his friends on their sleek blue urn, inching ever closer to Snorfo, zigzagging ahead on his chubby red one.

Turning his head to see the children approach, the duke growled and put on even greater speed. "Pardon my DUST!"

"Two can play that game!" said Neal. "Hold tight, everyone." He whispered a few words — "Nebbo-bo-shebbo!" — and the urn rolled completely over, then corkscrewed up over the streets. "Whoa-oa-oa!"

The duke turned around once more and gasped. "But where did you —"

Neal's urn dived back down again next to Snorfo's. "Peekaboo!" shouted Neal, digging his heels into the barrel of the urn and tightening his knees on its rim. He leaned left and knocked into Snorfo's urn, sending it wobbling away.

The duke nearly crashed into a balcony but managed to lean back in time and twist away to safety. When Neal pulled up over the balcony, his heart gave a flutter. The sun was low on the horizon. They had spent too long searching for the Medallion. In a couple of hours, the city would return to its bottle.

Nudging their urn to greater speed, Neal shortened the distance between them.

"Snorfo, you don't know what you're

doing!" called Keeah as they inched ahead. "The Medallion is far too powerful for you!"

"Mine!" cried Ing, who was suddenly back in the race. He appeared to be wearing a fresh diaper.

Neal grinned and glanced down to see Ming disposing of a white bundle.

Wrong move. In that fraction of a second, Snorfo twisted his urn around, came up behind the children, and snatched Neal's turban away. "Ha! Perfect fit! We *are* the same size!"

"Give that back!" shouted Neal as the word Neffu had used — "defenseless" — rang in his ears. "Give it!"

"Mmm, no," said Snorfo. "I like it —"

As if the turban gave him new intelligence, Snorfo fiddled with the three pieces of the Medallion. Suddenly, the children heard a distinct *click* and knew that one of the pieces was attached.

"No! Don't do that!" cried Max. "Snorfo, don't!"

There soon came a second *click*, and the three pieces were together.

"It's too much power for you!" said Julie.

Immediately, the air began to quake, and a beam shot up wildly from the Medallion.

"Ho-ho, lightning!" The duke laughed. "There's power for you!"

Then it came. A single sharp sound.

Crack!

Julie scoured the sky. "What was that?"

Keeah gasped. "My force field. The power of the Medallion, even incomplete, was too much for it. The shield has been broken!"

In seconds, it seemed as if the air in the entire City of Ut was being sucked away.

Ing, Ming, and Ving sank back to the square below, breathless, as the sound of heavy wings filled the air. Duke Snorfo brought his urn to a bumpy landing in the city's main square. He jumped off next to the obelisk and stared straight up. So did all the townspeople in the square.

The sky over the city went black, and the air filled with a deafening roar.

"What's happening?" asked Keeah.

Neal knew what was happening. How he knew, he couldn't say. But he did.

"Into the shadows!" he whispered. And the children and Dumpella scurried into the shadows to keep from being seen.

At that moment the sky filled with a thousand wingwolves. They swooped down and flooded the square around Snorfo, standing at attention as if waiting for someone.

Then that someone came.

A giant dragon with four jagged wings, a bony head, and fiery-red eyes.

"No," whispered Max. "Not . . . him . . ."

"Him!" said Dumpella.

"G . . . G . . . G . . ." stuttered Ving.

" . . . ethwing!" Ming finished.

"He scary," said Ing.

Landing on the cobblestones, Gethwing folded his great wings behind his shoulders. His long white fangs shone in the fading golden sun. He narrowed his fiery eyes and one by one searched the faces of the bystanders. The guards, the hawk creatures, the citizens of Ut, all froze where they stood.

All except Duke Snorfo.

Duke Snorfo didn't freeze.

He quaked uncontrollably.

Then he gasped.

Then he fell to the ground in a faint.

Eight

The Moon Dragon

With Gethwing only inches away, Neal wanted to run. Or fly. Or vanish.

Or even be back in math class.

But he couldn't budge from the shadows. Terror seemed to nail his orange curly-toed boots to the cobblestones, into the ground, through the earth, and out the other side.

We so do not need Gethwing here, he said.

No kidding, said Julie.

How did he know we were here? asked Keeah. *How did he find us?*

The dragon's heavy footsteps resounded like thunder over the cobblestones.

Circling Gethwing's bony head was the infamous crown known as the Coiled Viper.

Fashioned by Lord Sparr into the shape of a snake twined upon itself, the Viper had helped secure Neffu, Sparr, and Ungast to Gethwing, forming the moon dragon's Crown of Wizards.

As the dragon stared from face to face, the Viper's venomous eyes pulsed brightly.

"So this . . . is Ut," Gethwing said.

Breaking their silence, Ving and Ming stumbled over themselves to bow.

"Your wonderful dragonness!" said Ming. "Allow me to be the first —"

"Your dragony wonderfulness!" said Ving, grinning. "I am honored to be the first to —"

"Silence!" boomed Gethwing. "I came for one thing and one thing only."

To capture us? whispered Julie.

Worse, said Keeah. *He came for the Medallion. But how did he know it was here?*

"Me Ing!" said the smallest hawk creature, stepping forward, a drop of drool leaking from his beak. "Me Ing . . . ," he repeated.

"Hush, little one," said the dragon. "Hush."

"But me Ing . . . ," Ing wailed.

"Silence!" boomed Gethwing, and the baby's beak clacked shut.

"Did someone already say 'uh-oh'?" Neal whispered out of the side of his mouth.

"You just did," whispered Dumpella.

Neal nodded. "I can say that again!"

What struck Neal were not Gethwing's stern features or fearful words. They were normal for the moon dragon. What Neal noticed this time was that Gethwing seemed larger than he remembered. Much larger. His four giant wings, black and scalloped, were arched and more massive than ever. His arms looked as if they had been hewn out of stone and his claws forged from iron. With every breath Gethwing took, the horns on his head sizzled with black sparks that scattered and hissed on the cobblestones.

In two quick steps, the dragon stood over the turbaned form of Duke Snorfo. "Is this the pesky genie boy called Zabilac?" he asked.

Neal trembled. "Uh-oh. Again."

"He got muffin hat!" said Ing, scratching his beak.

"So, Zabilac," said Gethwing, towering over the unmoving form, "how fare your little genie tricks now?"

With a single swift move, Gethwing snatched the Medallion from Snorfo's grasp.

Are you kidding me? said Julie silently. ***How many times will the Medallion change hands today?***

Gethwing bent his giant head to the silver object. He examined its front and back, touching it gently with his claws.

"This . . . is incomplete," he growled. "It is missing Lord Sparr's piece, the Twilight Star!"

With that, the dragon raised his claws to the sky and howled in rage. At once, a flash of light streaked across the sky, and a golden chariot harnessed to a pair of black groggles zigzagged down to the main square, with Princess Neffu at the reins.

And Neffu, too! said Keeah. **How did they all know the Medallion was in Ut?**

"I must have the complete Medallion," Gethwing growled, scanning the square once more. "Whoever prevents me from having it will live to regret it — but not for very long!"

"No preventing," said Ming. "No, no!"

"No regretting, either," said Ving.

We need to stall for time, said Keeah. **Neal? Julie? Any thoughts?**

Neal became aware of someone kicking his foot. As usual, it was Dumpella.

"Nealie, now's your chance," she whispered. "Be the duke. Be Snorfo!"

"Too dangerous," whispered Max. "Neal will be torn to shreds without his turban."

Neal gulped. But he knew Dumpella was right. "I have no choice," he whispered.

"I have to slow Gethwing down. I'm going —"

"Wait," said Julie, holding his arm. "I'm going with you."

Neal smiled. **Thanks. You be Dumpella and I'll be Snorfo.**

Better than the other way around, she said.

Good luck, said Keeah. **Dumpella, Max, and I will be with you . . . invisibly.**

With that, she cast a handful of dust over herself and the others, and they faded into the shadows.

Neal felt as though he were starring in the school play and couldn't remember a single one of his lines. But he puffed up his chest and strode out of the shadows. With Julie by his side, he swaggered up to Gethwing. He shouted in Snorfo's usual style. "HELLO, dragon! Looks like YOU CAUGHT THE SILLY GENIE BOY!"

Gethwing swiveled his head and brought it inches away from Neal's nose, which still stung in the spot where he'd struck the vanishing tower.

"Actually," said the dragon, "I did."

Actually, you didn't, Julie said to Neal, even as she curtsied to Gethwing. "O great four-winged terror guy, welcome to our city in a bottle."

Gethwing's eyes were as icy as ever. "To conquer Jaffa City, I require the greatest magical devices in Droon. The Moon Medallion is one of those. The *complete* Medallion!"

Eric needs it, too, Neal said silently.

"Where is the Twilight Star?" asked Gethwing.

Neal knew that Snorfo had the Star in his secret room in the palace tower. "It's hidden in a SAFE PLACE!" he said.

"The very safest place!" Julie added.

"Show me!" Gethwing boomed, practically knocking them over with his foul dragon breath. "Show me now. Where is it?"

Neal knew he needed to stall the dragon until he could think of a way to stop him. "I hid the Twilight Star . . . UNDER THE OBELISK!"

And he gestured toward the stone column in the center of the square.

But . . . , Julie said.

I think I'm having an idea, said Neal.

Go with it! said Julie.

Gethwing growled under his breath. "Hawks, while I retrieve the object, take the genie boy to the dungeon. The worst dungeon in this entire bottle."

"The worst dungeon . . . is UP THERE!" Neal said, pointing to the purple tower. "Take the boy . . . THERE!"

Gethwing smiled. "Good. The genie

needs a lesson taught to him. The harsher, the better."

"Aye, aye," said Ving.

"Aye, aye, aye!" said Ming.

Ing looked over his shoulder and sniffed.

"Before you TAKE HIM away," said Neal, "there's JUST ONE THING!" With care he slipped his turban off of Snorfo's head and set it on his own. "I LIKE THIS HAT!"

"I'll bet you do," said Neffu with a grin.

While Ving and Ming carried the unconscious duke off to the tower, Neal and Julie led the dragon slowly over to the obelisk. A troop of wingwolves followed them.

When they arrived at the column, the dragon turned to Neal. "Show me the Twilight Star, and I shall leave you to your . . . bottle."

"THANK you," said Neal.

"But first," said Gethwing, eyeing Neffu, then searching the two children's faces, "let me ask you a tiny question —"

"ASK AWAY!" said Neal.

"How long have you been a genie?"

"Not long," said Neal. "Only a few . . ."

Oh, Neal! Julie groaned.

Neal cleared his throat. "I mean . . . how long have I been *what*?"

"Impostor!" bellowed Gethwing, his claws sizzling with black sparks. "*Zabilac!* I knew it was you ever since Neffu placed a certain black jewel on your turban."

"What?" asked Neal. "She placed a . . ." Then he remembered Neffu's strange attack at Silversnow. He tore off his turban, spotted the black jewel, and pulled it off, hurling it to the ground.

Neffu laughed coldly. "Why do you think I came to Silversnow? For the weather?"

Neal groaned. "What a dummy I am!"

"Oh, no," said Gethwing, his eyes flashing. "A dummy has more sense than you do. Give me the Twilight Star now!"

Everything was happening at once. Neal grew hot and confused and nervous. It was like math class all over again. "No!" he said.

Gethwing slowly shook his gigantic head. "Even a dummy knows not to cross me. Neffu, take the girl! This one's mine!"

The dragon lunged at him. Neffu lunged at Julie.

Neal felt as if his head would explode. "I — can't — take — it!" he screamed.

Pulling his turban low on his head, he shouted at the top of his lungs, "*STOP!*"

And all at once, everything *did* stop.

Completely, utterly, and totally.

Nine

The Cave of Night

Neal realized he had been holding his breath only when he finally let it go and gulped in a huge lungful of air.

Everyone in the square had stopped moving. Stopped screaming. Stopped breathing.

"Holy cow . . . ," he whispered.

Gethwing's dark shape was completely airborne, leaping at where Neal had been. His great jaws were frozen in a howl, drops of venom hanging at a standstill between his fangs. His eyes were caught in a flash of rage.

"I like you better like this," Neal mumbled.

Julie was twisted away from Neffu and jumping for the sky, both feet off the ground.

Neffu's face was frozen in a scowl.

"Typical," he whispered.

Behind them, the wingwolves were motionless, each one arched in the air, their eyes like black marbles, their wolfen odor frozen around them like a cloud.

"Uck," he said.

Looking at everyone stopped in mid-move, Neal had the tiniest worry that he couldn't start things going again. Bracing his feet on the ground, he adjusted his turban.

"*MOVE!*" he shouted.

Sound roared. Gethwing leaped. Julie screamed.

"Okay, *STOP!*" he cried.

Everything stopped as it had before, like a film caught in midframe.

"Good. Fine," Neal said.

Using all his strength, he tried to unclamp Gethwing's grip from the Moon Medallion, but the dragon's claws were as hard as iron sealed in cement. They wouldn't budge.

Neal tried again and again. Nothing. He slumped to the ground. "So now what?"

Realizing he needed to ask someone for advice, but finding no one around, he had a conversation with himself.

"I need help."

"I sure do."

"But I'm already a genie. Where do genies get help?"

"From other genies?"

"Good idea!"

"I wouldn't have thought of it without you."

"Gosh, you're the best."

"No, you are."

And that was how Neal decided to call on the genies. Searching his scroll, he discovered the ancient spell used to find the other Genies of the Dove. He uttered the spell.

"Salla-malla-palla-boo!"

With the last syllable still on his lips, he felt everything spin as if he stood at the center of a merry-go-round that revolved faster and faster. Every color and shape blurred together like watercolors left out in the rain, until all of a sudden — *thunk!* — the spinning stopped, and Neal found himself in a gigantic cave. The ceiling seemed as far away as the sky and the walls no nearer than a distant horizon.

"Genies?" he whispered.

"Hush," said a voice Neal recognized instantly as belonging to his old friend Hoja. "You found us in the legendary Cave of Night. We're on a mission. To help you!"

"Where is the Cave of Night?" asked Neal.

"No one knows," said Anusa from somewhere behind him. "This is a shadow vision of a place only Gethwing himself knows."

"It is the place of his birth," said Fefforello.

"Gethwing tricked me into bringing him right to Ut," Neal told them. "And now he has the Moon Medallion!"

"That is why we're here," said Fefforello, flicking a handful of light crystals into the air.

Now able to see, Neal zigzagged carefully across the rocky floor of the cave and pressed his way forward as if familiar with it.

"Have I ever done this before?" he asked.

"Genies often feel this way," said Jyme. "When you travel through time as much as we do, what is done for the very first time often seems quite familiar."

The twin babies Stream and River floated overhead. They hadn't learned to walk yet.

"Mibble-dibble?" they asked.

"True, we are close," said Anusa.

All at once, a sound echoed in the darkness behind them. Another. And another. And the floor came alive with the sound of wet slithering. Small, featureless creatures with long thin arms, smooth skin, and faces as pale as the moon rose from the cave floor.

"Goblins!" hissed Anusa.

"But if this is a vision," said Neal, "how can the goblins bother us?"

"They are *shadow* goblins," said Hoja. "They live only in dreams and visions. Gethwing has armed his secret cave with great defenses!"

"We're too close to stop now!" said Jyme. "We'll deal with the goblins. Zabilac, go. Learn Gethwing's secret —"

As more and more goblins slithered out of the deep shadows, Neal turned and ran.

"Zabilac, hurry!" said Anusa.

Pushing ahead into the darkness, Neal felt a separation, like the place where two halves of a curtain meet. He pushed through. The space beyond was even darker than the cave, but he made out a large stone wheel, three feet thick, lying flat on the ground, turning soundlessly.

Going still, he watched the wheel turn and turn until another voice sounded in his ear.

The voice was so familiar, Neal was almost certain it was his own, only it came from outside him. Yet it *was* his own voice.

Turning, Neal saw himself, older, *much* older, and he knew that it was Zabilac, the old genie he would someday become.

Or had once been.

He wasn't quite sure.

"Hey," said his older self.

"Hey," Neal replied.

Even grown-up and old, Zabilac still had thick blond hair, though it was tinged with a few strands of gray — as well as green, violet, and red! The enormous blue turban — the same one Neal had on his head right then —was perched at a jaunty angle like a giant blueberry, although it was strung with many more jewels, each one glowing brightly.

Man, I look good! thought Neal.

I can hear you, by the way, said the older man. **But thanks.**

Neal laughed. "What is that wheel thing?"

Zabilac frowned. "This is Gethwing's life wheel. As long as it turns, the dragon lives."

"It's huge," said Neal. "It must be ten feet from the outside to the middle."

"Right, the diameter," Zabilac whispered.

Neal turned. "Wait. I know that word."

Zabilac smiled. "Julie told us, don't you remember? To find out how big around the stone is, you multiply the diameter — ten feet — by pi, which is 3.1416."

"Julie was trying to explain it!" said Neal. "I can't believe there's another kind of pie."

Zabilac kept smiling. "So what is the circumference of the wheel — the length around the entire edge?"

Neal went over the numbers in his head. "Ten feet times 3.1416 . . . is 31.42 feet?"

"That's how pi works," said Zabilac.

"*Pie*," said Neal.

"Yes," said Zabilac, as if reading Neal's thoughts. "But there's no *e* at the end."

Neal smiled. "Got it."

But his smile faded as the wheel turned and turned and turned. "I think it's getting faster. What does that mean?"

"That Gethwing's not nearly done," said Zabilac. "Not for a long time."

Neal stepped to the wheel. The instant he let his fingers touch the turning stone, his brain flashed with a thousand images, and his ears roared with the howl of the dragon.

Neal saw a silver medallion, a girl swimming in a lake, a trio of wizards flying in the morning sky. He saw his friends as he first knew them, young and small, and then as if decades had gone by, and they were old and stumbling, and finally gray and still. He saw a thorn-haired queen laughing in a wreath of flames, and a blue serpent becoming a blue airplane in the blink of an eye. He saw a small child sitting in a silver tree and then another tree growing from a tomb and then hundreds of pilkas stampeding across the desert and a single candle's flame flickering in the night.

Finally, he saw a gleam of silver light fall from a great distance upon that turning wheel, and Gethwing himself and a boy in purple armor by his side. He heard the chanting of words as of a prophecy, words and words and words. Seven hands reached toward one another in the darkness and came to rest upon that wheel.

Then he saw nothing.

With a force like a powerful wave, Neal was tossed back from the stone wheel, and the vision was gone as quickly as it had come.

"Whoa!" said Neal, staggering to his feet. "What *was* all of that?"

Zabilac searched the boy's face before answering. "That, Neal, is your power."

"I saw seven hands on the wheel," Neal said. "What does it mean?"

"Seven people must join to stop the wheel. Only then will Gethwing be defeated."

Neal wondered if his own hand was among the seven. "The seven genies?"

Zabilac studied the wheel, then shook his head. "Only you have made it this far.

The King of Genies can go where others cannot."

"Cool," said Neal. "But you're the king."

"And I . . . am you," said the older genie. "You are king. You, Neal. But there's other stuff, too. Not so cool. Or . . . not cool in the same way."

"What kind of stuff?" asked Neal.

"Sometimes being a king, even King of Genies, means you have to take on what no one else should," said the older man. "Sometime, maybe soon, you'll feel a hurt beyond what you think you can bear."

Neal thought of Eric. Was it Eric with Gethwing at the wheel? The boy in purple?

"But sometimes," the man said, "it's a pain that will help. Some of what I mean involves another wheel of life. A much bigger one."

Neal trembled inside. "Whose is it? Eric's?"

"It's the wheel of Droon," Zabilac said.

"Is it speeding up? Or slowing down?"

Zabilac turned to him. Neal felt that looking at him was like gazing into a magic mirror. The older genie opened his lips to speak, when Hoja yelled from beyond the curtain.

"Zabilac! Time to go! Zabilac?"

"He means you," said the older man.

"But what about Droon's wheel? Is it slowing down, is it ending, or not?"

"I . . . cannot . . . say," said the older genie.

"Zabilac!" cried Hoja.

Taking one last look at Gethwing's wheel, Neal left his older self and pushed his way out of the darkness. The genies had defeated the goblins and were waiting by the cave entrance. But their eyes were full of fear.

"Gethwing's armies are approaching Ut," said Anusa. "We must go at once."

"But I stopped everything," said Neal.

Anusa shook her head. "Genie powers can stop things only in a certain place. The rest of the world keeps moving."

"Luckily, we know what to do," said Hoja. "You remember that the City of Ut connects through the center of the earth to the Doom Gate under the Serpent Sea."

"At the obelisk," said Neal.

Fefforello nodded. "The Doom Gate is the ultimate prison. We shall bind the dragon and send him into the Doom Gate . . . forever!"

"Are you kidding? That sounds perfect!" said Neal. "Maybe the war will be over before it even begins."

"We can only hope," said Jyme.

"All ready?" said Hoja.

"Flibbie-ibbie!" said River and Stream.

The genies stood side by side in a ring with Neal, arms woven together like a garland.

"We're ready on your command, Zabilac," said Hoja.

"All hail, King of Genies!" said Jyme.

Neal's heart fluttered to hear the word king spoken by the genies one after another. But there was no time to linger. "Genies, to Ut!"

At once, the Cave of Night faded to a fine mist and fell to the ground like a dropped cloth. The cobblestones of Ut's vast courtyard took its place. Everyone was as Neal had left them, completely still, frozen, motionless.

"Shall we start everything going again?" asked Anusa, and all eyes looked to Neal.

"Just one thing," he said. "I've wanted to do this for a long time. I need a chain."

Hoja crossed his arms, and a length of silver chain appeared in Neal's hands.

He smiled. "Perfect!"

Tiptoeing to Gethwing, Neal wrapped the chain around his tail and tied the other end to the base of the obelisk. He tugged it once or twice, then smiled, satisfied.

"And now," he said, *"MOVE!"*

Ten

The Battle in the Bottle

No sooner had Neal spoken than Gethwing resumed his leap across the air. He flew like an arrow from a bow. Like a shot from a cannon. Like Neal from math class.

Until the chain pulled taut around his tail, and his leap was over. Shrieking at the top of his lungs, Gethwing fell with a resounding *thud*, causing the Moon

Medallion to fly out of his grasp and slide across the courtyard.

"THANK YOU!" said Neal, scooping it up.

At the same time, the genies surrounded Neffu and plopped her back into her chariot, securing her there with a second chain.

Gethwing staggered to his feet, foaming at the mouth like an angry dog. He broke the chain tying his tail to the obelisk, and it bounced across the stones like a whip. "Wingwolves, attack the turban heads!"

"No, you don't!" cried Keeah, reappearing with Max and Dumpella. "Neal, Julie, we're with you!"

Neal's heart thundered. "Genies, we'll take on the wolves. Do your stuff!"

"Aye, aye, King Zabilac!" said Hoja.

Neal's six fellow genies raised their hands, and sparks shot from one to the other, forming a giant battering ram. With one punch they burst the disc in the center of the square. Flames shot out of the hole that led straight through the earth to the Doom Gate.

"Bind the dragon; send him into the earth!" cried Anusa.

At once, a hundred chains materialized and spun around the dragon until he was covered head to foot with leaden bonds. Still struggling, the dragon managed to utter a command. "Neffu, trap the turban-headed boy at all costs. He has the Medallion!"

Neffu twisted once, and the chains binding her exploded. "I will!"

"You'll have to find us first!" said Neal. "Guys, to the palace and the Twilight Star!"

Neal and his friends charged out of the square. "This way! This way!" called Dumpella. "Escaping is fun! I like it!"

"They don't," said Julie as a dozen wolves swooped out of the sky, their claws flashing.

Keeah spun on her heels and sent a spray of sparks at the incoming wolves. They howled as the sparks singed their fur.

"My turn!" Neffu shrieked. Twisting the reins, she dived her chariot at them, hurling blasts of sizzling red sparks. Stones exploded at their feet as the children fled.

"Don't worry, Nealie," said Dumpella. "I know these streets like the pattern of the tiles in the main courtyard behind the palace." With a running leap, she dived over a low wall. Neal, Julie, Keeah, and Max followed and found themselves racing from one street to another, cutting through shops, leaping over fences, and crawling through gardens into a street of more shops.

"This looks familiar," said Max.

"Go left!" called the frog-faced shop owner from before. "And thanks for the nice tip!"

"Thank *you!*" said Keeah.

Turning left brought the kids into a neighborhood of streets so narrow and houses so close together that the wolves were forced to abandon the chase.

"How wonderful," said Max. "Now, Dumpella, show us to the tower —"

"Yoo-hoo! Don't forget about me!" snarled a voice.

All at once, they heard the familiar squeal of chariot wheels.

"Not Neffu already?" said Neal.

That sound was followed by the flapping of wings.

"And the hawk bandits?" said Julie.

"Not so fast, kidlings!" said Neffu, blocking the street ahead of them. "It would be better for you if you handed over the Medallion right now."

"You mean it would be better for *you*," said Keeah, just as the hawk bandits fluttered down and cut off escape the other way.

"Give us the shiny thing, or else!" said Ving.

"Me want it — now!" said Ing.

"No!" said the five friends together.

"Everyone . . . down!" said Keeah.

As everyone ducked, Keeah spun around, sending a spray of violet sparks in all directions. The hawk bandits were knocked back, and Neffu collapsed into a heap.

With a quick right and a left, Dumpella led the friends right into the purple palace.

"Upstairs!" she said. "To Snorfo and the Twilight Star. We need them both!"

They jumped from stairway to stairway until they were in Snorfo's room at the tower summit.

"Brother," said Dumpella, barging in, "we need the Twilight Star. You have to help us."

Snorfo lay on a mountain of cushions and pillows. He sighed. "What's the use? I want magic more than anything. But I can't defend myself against all of you. Take everything. I'm done."

"Where's the Star?" asked Max.

"Find it yourselves," said Snorfo.

Neal remembered his days without magic. He decided to give the duke a reason to help them. "Snorfo, do you like to fly?"

Duke Snorfo perked up his ears. "More than anything!"

Neal turned to an urn by the door. He whispered some words over it, and it began to float. "You don't need the Twilight Star for this. It's your own private flying urn!"

Snorfo jumped onto the urn and flew it around the room. "Yes, yes, yes! Here —"

He tugged a small iron chest out and, using a very large key, he opened it. The Twilight Star spun magically before them.

"Yes!" cried Neal. He took the Star in one hand, removed the Moon Medallion from a pouch on his belt, and joined the pieces.

Click! The room beamed with sudden silver light. At the same time, a thunderous sound came from below, and the children scrambled out to the tower ramparts and looked down.

Bound in chains from his tail to his head, Gethwing writhed in pain. He lay in the great hole that led all the way from Ut to the Doom Gate on the far side of the world.

"Thrust the dragon down!" cried Anusa. "Seal him from our world forever!"

Neal couldn't take his eyes away from what his genie friends were doing. "Holy moly!"

"Our eyes do not deceive us," chirped Max. "The defeat of the Moon Dragon comes — now!"

Neal's heart thudded against his chest.

"It's working," he said. "People, we're winning. Even while Gethwing struggles, we're winning. We *won't* have a war in three days. We may already have won. Droon will soon be free!"

He turned to Keeah. "Earlier today, you sent the message that you needed us *now*. Now. At first I thought you meant we *won*. Now I think that was a glimpse of the future. Because here and now I think we *have* won —"

Then . . . something happened.

Thip . . . thip . . .

Neal shuddered. "Oh, no . . ."

"What's wrong?" said Keeah. "We have the Medallion. Gethwing is trapped. We can go. We can go —"

"No," said Neal. "Someone else is . . . here."

Thip . . . thip . . .

It was the person who had been following them since they arrived in Ut.

Like a streak of dark light, the shape raced across the city wall. It flitted over the rooftops and right up to the summit of the purple tower where they stood.

As he watched, Neal suspected that in his heart he had known who it was from the first moment he heard his footsteps.

A boy materialized on the tower ramparts with them.

It was Prince Ungast.

Eleven

On the Purple Tower

Prince Ungast!

The moment the boy removed his heavy purple helmet, Neal felt his heart sink.

Eric was so changed from the last time he had seen him! His old friend seemed like a ghost. Eric's face was thin and gray with eyes that looked out with a hollow stare. He was no more than a shadow that lurked around the dark prince, like a rag of clothing Ungast would soon cast off, and Eric would be lost.

Lost forever.

For the third time that day, everything that had ever happened between Neal and his friend flashed through his mind.

The moment he and Eric had first met.

The time they got stuck in the tree outside his house and met Julie. The countless doughnuts they had shared. The day they first went down the rainbow stairs. The moment they saw Droon. Every moment since.

Neal wrenched himself loose from his thoughts and stepped toward his friend.

"Eric," he said. "Eric —"

Ungast's black eyes were so unlike his friend's. They turned on Neal as if on an enemy. He waved his curved blade coldly.

"Not another step," he growled.

Keeah's breath, close to Neal's ear, was labored, gasping. Standing next to Dumpella and Snorfo, Julie didn't seem to be breathing at all, while Max shifted from foot to foot, his great spider eyes widening.

"Eric?" said Keeah.

"Eric," Julie repeated.

The dark prince's eyes moved slowly over the staring faces, searching them for something they couldn't identify. They finally came to rest upon the silver object in Neal's hand.

"The Moon Medallion," he whispered. "That's what I've come for."

Neal held the Medallion tight. "But . . ."

"I'll take it," Ungast said sharply, raising his sword threateningly. "And Jaffa City will collapse into the dust it used to be."

Keeah stepped to him. "Eric, I thought —"

The dragon howled from the ground below.

Glancing down, Neal watched as chain after magical chain wound around Gethwing, until he grew almost still under the weight. He moaned more plaintively with each passing moment.

The dark prince moved his blade toward Keeah. "You . . . you . . ."

Ignoring the sword, Keeah took another step. "Listen, Eric," she said, "all this time, we've been hoping — *I've* been hoping — that you were still you. The words you said to me. Your request for the Medallion. I thought — we all thought —"

"Eric?" said the boy. "I'm not Eric . . . not anymore. That name is . . . wrong. . . ."

The last ray of sunlight sliced across the tower. To Neal, the dark prince seemed larger than before. Had Ungast grown while Eric diminished, as Gethwing himself had? Is that what happened when the good in you faded? The evil grew stronger, more powerful?

"I came here, drawn by the Medallion," Ungast said. "Give it to me, or I'll —"

"We *will* give it to you," said Neal, clasping the silver object to his chest. "You told us to, and we will."

"I don't remember telling you," said the prince, his sword lowering until it fell to his side.

"Maybe it wasn't the Medallion that drew you here," said Keeah. "Maybe you knew *we* would be here. Your friends. The ones who care about you. Maybe you were following us."

The prince shook his head as if to shake off her words. "No. Give me the Medallion!"

Neal held it tight. "We'll give this to you, but not until *you* become *you* again."

The prince's eyes flickered. "What?"

"The Medallion is not for Ungast," said Julie. "It's for Eric. Our friend Eric."

This time, the prince turned his head away as if the name meant something, as if it rang a distant bell in his mind. When a sound came from below, Ungast glanced over the balcony to where the giant dragon lay. Gethwing's fiery eyes stared toward the tower's top.

"Don't look at the beast," said Max. "Don't meet his glance."

With a single swift movement, Neal pushed his hand inside Ungast's heavy cloak and drew out the wrinkled photograph of the aviator and his plane. "Look at it," he said, holding the picture steadily in front of his friend. "Look at the picture.

Your mother wanted you to have this. As a reminder."

Ungast stared at the picture. "A reminder? Of what?"

"That man is your ancestor," said Keeah. "But only you really know what this photograph means."

Neal imagined he saw a flicker of recognition in Eric's eyes. "You wouldn't keep the picture unless some of Eric was still in you."

On the ground below, Gethwing moaned, his giant back crushed under the chains.

The genies prepared to lower the stone disc over Gethwing, sealing him in the earth.

"We have him!" cried Fefforello, dancing on the colored cobblestones of the square. "The dragon succumbs to the Doom Gate!"

Ungast turned his face away from the Moon Dragon. He shook his head. "I . . ."

"Gethwing is caught. Take the cure," said Keeah. She removed the vial from around her neck. "Become Eric — become your true self once more. Drink it now. All of it."

Keeah wrapped her hands around Ungast's, which, like his face, were as gray as death. She helped him hold the silver vial. She helped him raise it to his lips.

Ungast did this tentatively at first, then more eagerly, draining the contents of the vial. Soon the liquid was gone.

In moments, his gray features softened; color returned to his cheeks, breath to his chest, and sparkle to his eyes.

Time seemed to stop as it had before for Neal. But this time he knew his friends sensed the moment enveloping them, too.

They were all together for the first time in so many days.

Then, as if despite himself, Eric shuddered all over. Dropping his sword, he covered his face with his hands, burst into tears, and sank into his friends' embrace like a long-lost brother.

"Eric!" said Keeah. "Eric, Eric . . ."

Minutes passed, and when his tears had finally ebbed, Eric Hinkle was himself again.

"Dude!" said Neal. "It's been too long!"

"I can't believe this, any of it," Eric said. "It seems like centuries have passed while I've been inside this evil body, this dark mind."

"Take this," said Neal, handing him the Moon Medallion. "You asked for it. You need it to finish Gethwing once and for all."

"You're . . . free . . . ," said Julie softly.

But at the mention of the word free, Eric's face darkened. As if he remembered an obligation that he had, for just a moment, forgotten. He frowned. "Free . . . I don't know . . . no . . ."

Holding the Medallion in his hands, he pulled away from Neal and Julie and Keeah. Neal saw that he was shaking. His face was a mask of worry. Of pain. Of fear.

"What is it?" Keeah asked. "Gethwing is captured. The genies have trapped him. He is moments away from being sealed away forever —"

Eric breathed out slowly. "Is he? Is he really?"

"What do you mean?" asked Julie. "Look at him —"

"No, *you* look at him," said Eric.

As Eric spoke, they felt the tower shake with a thunderous *boom*. The giant obelisk exploded into a thousand pieces.

"What —" gasped Julie.

"Ungast!" the dragon howled.

Still wrapped in chains, Gethwing staggered out of the hole. With a thrust of his iron tail, he hurled the genies across the square and pushed away the remains of the stone obelisk as if they were nothing. Still bound, Gethwing staggered to the base of Snorfo's tower. He thrust a claw out of the web of chains and grasped the tower stones.

"What?" said Neal. "No. No!"

"Ungast!" the dragon cried. "I come!"

Trembling in the prince's suit of armor that was now far too large for him, Eric stared at the dragon.

"He's not finished," he said. "He has more to do! Gethwing is getting free. And he's coming . . . for me!"

Twelve

Behold the King

"Ungast!" Gethwing cried again.

Straining his massive muscles, the dragon planted his feet at the base of the tower and breathed in. His chest expanded, and one by one the magical silver chains began to snap.

"No!" yelled Hoja.

Anusa cried out, "Genies, to me! King Zabilac!"

"Eric, come with us," said Keeah, her

fingers sparking. "We need you. Right now. And we have to get out of here —"

Eric did not acknowledge her words.

Neal watched the chains snap and curl away from Gethwing as if they were no stronger than rubber bands. With his arms free, the dragon took hold of the massive stone disc and thrust it over the hole.

"I am not gone, not dead, not defeated!" Gethwing shouted, and Neal remembered the wheel of life, and the word that Zabilac had used, and it pierced his heart.

King. King Zabilac. King. King.

"Eric?" Keeah said. "What's going on?"

Her friend did not respond.

"Eric," Julie said. "You have the Medallion. You asked for it. We found it. And now you have it. We can stop Gethwing now. Come with us. Be with us again —"

The tower shook as Gethwing grasped the stones and dragged himself up the side.

"I . . . I . . . can't, can I?" said Eric. "Can I really come with you? Don't I have to stay with the dragon?"

"Neal, tell him," said Julie. "Tell him!"

Neal's eyes met Eric's and there was a moment when he wished with all his heart that he were somewhere else. Anywhere else.

But he was not anywhere else.

He was here.

And what he had seen when he touched Gethwing's wheel meant one thing to him. Eric was with the dragon to the very end.

"You have to stay with him," said Neal.

"He *what*? No! Stay with him?" said Julie, holding Eric's arm tightly. "I won't let you!"

"Genie or no genie, Neal," said Max, "Eric cannot stay with Gethwing. You see what it's doing to him. He must come with us! Now!"

"There is a secret," said Neal.

"Enough secrets!" said Keeah angrily. "This is crazy. Eric, we need to stop the dragon here and now. And we need you to do it!"

Gethwing howled from down below, and it was as if both boys, friends forever, knew at the same time.

Eric turned and placed his hands on Keeah's shoulders. "That's just it. We *can't* stop Gethwing now. Look at him down there. So close to being captured, then freeing himself. I realize something now I never knew. Something no one knew. Look at him!"

They saw the wounded dragon, his limp wings dragging behind him like ragged cloths, scale his way, stone by stone, up the side of the tower toward the top.

"I don't know why," Eric said, shaking his head, "but five times over the last few days, Gethwing has escaped death. I don't know how."

Neal's mind moved like an arrow from thought to thought. It moved to places he never knew were there. Finally, the arrow hit its mark, and his heart ached to understand the meaning of the wheel.

It was speeding up.

Gethwing was not done.

"Gethwing is . . . immortal," said Neal. "I had a glimpse of . . . something . . . a vision. There are words. A prophecy about him. About his wheel of life. And he is there and Eric is there. At the end." His eyes met Eric's and he knew they both knew he had to stay with Gethwing.

Eric turned. "I have to go."

"No," Keeah said, with a gasp. "No —"

"Neal is right," said Eric. "You're seeing Gethwing's power right now. Look at him!"

One after another, Gethwing's black wings unfurled themselves and caught the wind. His great arms bent back to their positions and thickened. His claws gouged the stones. His horns grew tall and curved once more.

And he climbed still higher.

"If I can discover that prophecy," Eric said breathlessly, "we stand a chance. Droon stands a chance. That's why there were five days. That's why he didn't attack Jaffa City right away. A prophecy must come true first. A prophecy must come to pass in him. It happens in two days, and I have to be there."

Neal was unable to take his eyes off the approach of the dragon. The tower shook from side to side.

"Look," Eric went on, "I said I'd hold him off, and I will. But he won't be defeated today. Thanks to Neal, I understand why. The Medallion is part of the final battle. But I have to follow through, or nothing we've worked for will happen. We have to have someone near him. We have to have . . . me."

"But, Eric," Keeah said, her eyes moist with tears. "How can we let you leave us again? We won't let you. *I* won't let you." She put her hand on his arm and held tight.

"You *have* to help me," Eric said, placing his hand over hers. "If you keep asking me, I'll come with you. But everything will be lost."

Neal thought of Eric's parents, how they missed their son, and he knew their pain because it was his own.

Julie's face was wet with tears, too. "It's so hard to hear you say this. . . ."

Eric shook his head. "We haven't seen how hard it will be. Even with all of us, even with the Moon Medallion. Even with Galen and all the millions of Droon helping, Gethwing can still win. He *will* win, unless I am with him. Two more days are all we have."

Pulling away from his friends, turning his face away from their faces, Eric bowed his head, donned Ungast's purple helmet, closed his eyes, and breathed once.

To Neal, seeing Eric leaving them once again hurt as much as it had the first time. No . . . it hurt more. He wanted to hold Eric back from what he was going to do.

But he knew he had to let him go.

It was the pain Zabilac had told him of.

The pain that hurt beyond hurting.

The pain that would help.

Eric closed his eyes — as much to stanch his tears as to call up a power — and began speaking ancient words, and he grew into the dark armor once more. He looked as Prince Ungast had looked moments before.

Halfway up the tower, Gethwing howled. "Ungast! Dearer than my own son to me!"

"You've given *me* the strength," Eric said to his friends, donning his helmet. "Now *you're* going to have to be strong. I want you to push me off the tower."

"You want *what*?" said Keeah. "No —"

"It's too tall," said Dumpella. "You'll never survive."

"You have to," Eric said. "And it has to look real. He's coming. Push me. Push me!"

"If this is what being the genie king means, I don't want it," said Neal.

"Yes, you do," said Eric. "We need you, Neal. Droon needs you, King of Genies."

Neal remembered seeing the hand-prints on Gethwing's wheel of life. And he knew with certainty that one of them was his own.

The dragon was close enough to see them now. "Ungast!"

"Sorry about this . . . ," said Eric, his eyes flashing as if in anger, though in his heart Neal knew it was the opposite.

With Ungast's sword raised, Eric leaped at Keeah. Neal had no choice but to block the thrust. He lunged at his friend and knocked him down with the lightest touch he could manage. It was enough.

Taking one more roll than he needed to, Eric tumbled off the edge of the balcony.

"Noooo!" Gethwing wailed as the greatest jewel in his Crown of Wizards

plummeted to the ground. With a show of his awesome strength, the dragon spread his wings, leaped off the side of the tower, and dived for Eric.

He caught the boy seconds before he struck the ground, then swooped back into the air.

As he did, Eric stared at his friends, the Moon Medallion safely hidden in the secret pocket of his cloak, next to the mysterious old photograph.

Two days more are all we have! said Eric. *Find Galen! We need him now! Go. Go!*

Gethwing swept up into the air. "Princess Neffu, wingwolves, join me now! We go!"

"No kidding!" yelled Neffu. "I'm not getting stuck here for a whole century!"

And go they did. With a whirl of black wind, the evil forces soared over the city and escaped as they had come, through the shattered force field.

"Ing go, too!" cried the baby hawk.

Ving and Ming scooped up their brother and flew away with the others.

Below, the six genies held hands in a circle and conjured the obelisk into place once more, sealing the Doom Gate as it had been.

"Whisper but the words, King Zabilac," called Hoja, "and we shall come!"

With that, the six genies faded into ghosts of themselves and vanished as before into the fields of time.

"We must go, too," said Max.

With few words, Julie, Keeah, and Max bade good-bye to Snorfo and Dumpella.

Neal took longer. For a moment, and another and another, Neal couldn't manage to express his thoughts.

"A quiet genie," said Dumpella. "I like that. I think I know what you mean. Don't be a stranger." She gave him a hug. A long hug.

"Time to go," said Julie, pulling him away.

All together, they escaped the high purple walls, just as the City of Ut vanished into its bottle once more.

The windswept plains were empty now, except for thousands of hoof tracks and the giant boot prints of the Silversnow knights.

The battle had moved on.

Moments later, the sun sank behind the mountains, and the plains grayed in the gathering twilight.

"Two days," said Neal. "We have our mission."

"And Eric has his," said Keeah.

"Let us meet in the morning," said Max. "Farewell until then."

"Tomorrow will come soon enough," said Julie. "Neal, the rainbow stairs. Come on."

As he raced Julie up the stairs to home, Neal felt that the secrets of Droon were more numerous and tangled than ever before. The stakes were vast, and danger approached from every direction.

But in his heart, his pained heart, Neal knew the solution was coming.

It was coming fast.